CW00738632

First published in 2017 by
Mabecron Books Ltd
Briston Orchard, St Mellion, Saltash, Cornwall, PL12 6RQ
United Kingdom. All rights reserved.
Illustrations Michelle Cartlidge

Typeset in Baskerville
Printed in Malta

ISBN 978 0 9955 0282-6

The Mousehole Mice
and the Theatre by the Sea

Michelle Cartlidge

M

Mabecron Books

*T*he morning sun sparkles on Mousehole harbour and the mouse family are here again for another lovely seaside holiday. This year they have a new baby mouse called Lola.

L ooking out across the beautiful harbour they see the big ship as it sails out
to the Islands for the day. They are excited to see Gardener Mouse with his
full wheelbarrow, and Fisher Mouse with his freshly caught mackerel.

I n the mouse restaurant, Fisher Mouse offers Chef his *catch of the day*.
Meanwhile the mouse family enjoy a wonderful breakfast as they plan
their day out. Father Mouse explains, 'Later this morning we will meet
Skipper in his boat on Mousehole quay and go on a sea journey to a very
special place - the Magical Theatre by the Sea.'

Strolling round the village, the mouse family meet a very happy, quacky, chatty little duck called Dylan. He is waddling around in a beautiful seaside garden, and he is so very sweet.

Lola and her big brother Jack and her big sister Molly spend time watching the little duck who tells them about the Mermice out in the bay.

Then it's time to head off and meet Skipper in his boat, down on Mousehole quay.

The mouse family are all aboard, and the little boat edges out through the narrow hole in the harbour wall. 'That's how Mousehole got its name,' explains Skipper, 'because it's like a real mouse hole.'

As the little boat follows the coastline, Mousehole behind them becomes smaller and smaller. It all looks so different from the sea.

On the way to the Theatre, the mouse family spot a beautiful sandy cove with a little wooden summer house built into a cave. There they can see some mouse friends relaxing, painting, and enjoying the sunshine. Some oystercatchers gather on the rocks nearby, picking through the seaweed looking for tasty morsels.

*T*hey all think the Theatre looks fantastic from the sea. Skipper waves goodbye and calls, 'Have a wonderful time and I'll meet you back here after the performance.' The mouse family wave back happily as they climb the winding coast path to reach the Theatre.

p at the Theatre, the mouse gardeners are busy planting and working hard to keep the gardens looking beautiful. Sometimes the weather is very wild up on the cliffs, so they need extra help from a few sprightly Mouse Garden Fairies who are flying about in the sunshine.

I n the dressing room, the mouse performers prepare to go onstage. 'You all look fantastic! Cool and fabulous, my darlings!' says the wardrobe mistress. 'Good luck for the performance. It's your 5-minute call. You have five minutes.'

Mouse Theatre by the Sea
proudly presents:

Mouse Summer
Dream,
A Fairytale Of Delight

written by
Sweet William Mouse

*T*he audience take up their places, the mouse family comfortably seated in the front row and the show begins...

The Mouse Fairy Dancers sweep across the stage, swirling and twirling, while Lucky, the Mouse Minstrel, plays the flute.

Princess Sunflower meets her Prince Sunshine. 'I have to depart on my travels for a while' he says, 'But soon I will return for you, my dear Princess.'

W ild Rose, the Mouse Witch, strides onto the stage with her three sparkly cats: Diamond, Ruby and Sapphire. They take up their stage positions around her, waiting for her command.

'You say the Prince will return,' she cackles.
And casts her witchery doubts.

'I don't know, I don't know.
These *mousey* fairytales of *mousey* hopes and *mousey* dreams.
Chance will be a fine thing!'

She swirls around the stage with her cats at her tail.
'Ha, Ha, Ha!' she cackles as the cats, 'Meow, Meow, Meow.'

From behind the stage Princess Sunflower hears it all,
'What a wicked witch ... I know my dear Prince will return.'

As the Princess sits pondering, the mouse audience are delighted to spot the Mermice splashing and dancing in the waves behind her.

And down below the cliff, unseen by the audience, the Mermouse Sea Queen sits on her Royal Rock throne. With her cod fish butler by her side, she watches the fabulous Mermice display.

Prince Sunshine does indeed return, and offers his hand of friendship to Princess Sunflower. She is delighted and proclaims, 'What more could any mouse princess ask for?'
Lucky plays the flute while the Mouse Fairies perform the Dance of the Sunflowers. The Prince and Princess begin their journey of...
happy times ~ happy days ~ and happy adventures.

All the cast come back onstage for the finale. The mouse audience loved the show and clap loudly. It has been a great success, but now it's time to leave the Magical Theatre by the Sea. The mouse family make their way back down the winding coast path to meet Skipper, who is waiting for them in his boat.

*A*rriving back again, after another exciting sea journey, Skipper ties the boat up alongside the quay.

It has been a wonderful trip to the Magical Theatre by the Sea, but it's nice to be back in Mousehole with the sound of herring gulls all around them.

The mouse family climb up the harbour wall steps to a lovely *welcome back* from Fisher Mouse and their special new friend Dylan, the little duck.

They make their way back to their holiday home in the village and the very happy, quacky little duck follows his new mouse friends all the way back to his seaside garden.